D1090354

# Amazing Abe Has Autism!

First Edition

Fulton Books, Inc.
Meadville, PA

Published by Fulton Books 2021

ISBN 978-1-63710-236-7 (paperback)
ISBN 978-1-63985-307-6 (hardcover)
ISBN 978-1-63710-237-4 (digital)

Printed in the United States of America

# Amazing Abe Has Autism!

Rooman F. Ahad, MD

To Ammi and Daddy, my guides who
encouraged me to reach for the stars.
To R and Z, my little loves and my inspiration.
To Z, for your support on this journey together.

Hello, my name is Abe!

I am three years old...
and growing smarter
every single day!

WELCOME OUR
NEW FRIEND ABE

I talk...very little right now, and sometimes people don't understand what I am saying.

But I understand...my mommy when she hugs me and my daddy when he kisses me. They love me!

I know I can do anything I dream of...
my mommy tells me this everyday.

I want to be able to tell my daddy I love him... I know I will do it soon.
da da!

I really love...watching my friends play. One day soon I will play with them too.

They call it...autism.
My friend, the speech
therapist, says I am
super special, kind,
and amazing.
B
A
K
X
Y

Will you...come on the special journey with me and watch me grow? I hope so!

# About the Author

Rooman's favorite activity to do after a long day is to cuddle up with her little ones and read a great book. When she began thinking of writing a children's book, she thought about the world in which she was raising her own children. She wanted to create awareness around special needs and autistic children.

Rooman is a board-certified child neurologist with a special interest and supplemental training in the field of autism and neurobehavioral disorders. She was born and raised in the city of Chicago. She started her pediatrics training at Advocate Lutheran General Hospital. Then she completed her neurology and autism training at the Johns Hopkins Hospital and Kennedy Krieger Institute in Baltimore. Rooman has always had an interest in writing children's books and sharing her experiences. She resides in Henderson, Nevada, with her husband and two children. When she isn't caring for her patients, she spends time with her family—baking, reading, collecting poetry, and travelling.